Island Views

Paula Johanson

Published by Doublejoy Books, 2020.

This is a work of fiction. Similarities to real people, places, or events are entirely coincidental.

ISLAND VIEWS

First edition. July 31, 2020.

ISBN: 978-1777144258

Written by Paula Johanson.

For Bernie - thanks for the adventures.

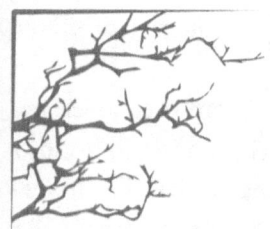

Island Views

The water was black, flat and glassy, with a curl where the bow wave rippled. The wave began as a swell a finger's width above the surface and grew as it was gradually left behind, until it broke and foamed and joined with the wake of the little ferry. The widening V of the wake spread out across Satellite Channel, and Elise saw where the wave from their passage minutes ago was now disturbing the small boats and yachts across the channel. Something about the way they bobbed without control disturbed her sense of balance, and she turned from the bright sails to look at the island looming up before the ferry. That was better!

"There's a road to the top of that mountain," said a voice over her shoulder. "You're smiling like you'd like to climb that mountain. I can drive you up that road and down it at a hundred klicks if you don't mind rolling at a couple of corners and banging against the rocks." Elise didn't jump at the sudden voice; nothing could startle her anymore after the boom of the ferry's horn.

"I think I'll pass on rolling down the mountain," she replied as she turned. "Tell me, does your car look any better than you do?" Elise looked him over quickly and wondered if he must be one of those island people her roommate had told her about, always at work fixing some project that kept him from real work.

"Car? My good woman, I do not own a *car*. This here is a Land Rover." He brushed at his grease-stained shirt. "This vehicle is the highest form in the evolution of the fossil fuel automobile and like any high performance vehicle it necessitates continual tuning to keep it in perfect running order. This accounts for my somewhat dishevelled appearance," he finished, wiping his hands on his jeans. "Dale Willis at your service."

"Elise Hammell at yours," she returned, and shook the proffered hand. "Are you always so formal?" She doubted it.

"Only when I'm filthy. Let me get a clean shirt from the Rover and I'll be the casual lech who tries to pick you up, offering an island holiday. THREE SUNLIT DAYS!" he roared, rummaging under the driver's seat with one hand. "Fourteen GLORIOUS nights in the HARBOURS and bistros of BEAUTIFUL Saltspring Island! EXPLORE the natural wonder of the island's ROCKS and trees. Or, for the more botanically inclined, TREES and rocks!" While talking, Dale shrugged out of his stained shirt and into a clean white t-shirt.

No one nearby appeared to be noticing him. Most of the other passengers were upstairs in the lounge playing gin rummy, or drinking machine-made coffee on the sun deck. Thank goodness! Elise was not interested in being pulled into a show on the car deck. "Do you always make a spectacle of yourself?" she asked, grinning in spite of herself. She had heard the same spiel at Disneyland's Jungle Boat Safari.

"Only when trying to impress somebody," Dale answered in a more honest tone. He tucked in the t-shirt and pulled his belt a little tighter around his narrow waist. "Tell me, Miss Hammell —"

"*Ms* Hammell," she said tightly, and let her eyes wander away from his flat stomach and ornate brass belt buckle.

"Tell me, Ms Hammell," he began again, unperturbed. "We've known each other for two whole minutes now and you've done nothing but ask me questions."

"Does that bother you?" Elise returned.

Dale marked a stroke on an imaginary blackboard. "A woman after my own heart. You've got one on me now."

"What happens when I get three on you?" Elise sketched a stroke on her own imaginary blackboard.

Dale stepped back, swayed by the ferry's slight rocking motion. "You get my services! Sunlit days and glorious nights touring my island home."

"I think I'll pass." Elise turned back to watch the dark water again. "Thanks, but I'm on a holiday. I don't intend to make it a pub crawl into the island's only pub."

"There are more pubs than that," Dale said in a tone of hurt pride. He came to stand at the rail with her as three seagulls flew up. White and grey, the two mature gulls caught the wind and hovered easily beside Elise, just out of arm's reach. The dappled grey youngster fell back and had to flap.

"That's not a selling point." Elise looked ahead and gestured with her chin. "Is that the dock?"

"Fulford Harbour. We'll be there in a few minutes. Have you made arrangements for when you arrive?"

"I think I can handle it," Elise said with some heat. "Hotels and luggage aren't exactly tricky." This conversation was beginning to wear on her. "Excuse me, I'm going back to my bags now. I want to be ready for when we dock." The gulls peeled away from the rail and the young one dropped back, unable to keep up. Elise walked back along the car deck to where she had left her knapsack and duffle bag beside a nest of ten-speed bicycles.

This vacation was turning out to be a lot of fresh air already. Going to an island of Sixties refugees might make meeting exciting new people unlikely, but Elise had heard about the potters and writers and artists on Saltspring. Surely she'd find some interesting people, especially if they crawled out of the woodwork like this guy Dale had. Too early to see yet if he was one of the eternal fixers, but she suspected it. She disliked to chat and flirt with a stranger when there was nothing to be done to put him off gently, but she'd rather spend an extra minute to talk someone out of an interest in her than simply tell him to get lost.

Those stomach muscles, though! *He must work out,* she thought. No one at her fitness club looked as good as that. *I'll have to ask him where he trains. How many places can there be on an island this size, anyways?*

PAULA JOHANSON

Maybe more places than she had assumed. The wash from the *Mayne Queen* was splashing up on shore as the ferry edged its way into the dock past wooden guides. Great beams of cedar ten inches thick had been bolted together to guide the ferry in towards the dock. Elise was staring at the parking lot on the other side of the dock when the ferry collided with the wooden guide. Splinters bristled from the great beams. A glancing blow, on a calm day. Shuddering at the impact, Elise grabbed the rail and looked at the splintered scars of previous collisions, then back to the parking lot. Were cars really needed on an island this small? Just how big was Saltspring, anyways?

Once the ferry had nudged into the dock at Fulford Harbour, a handful of people walked off from the front and up a ramp. Then vehicles left up the ramp, including a produce truck, a carpenter's half-ton pickup, and three electric cars full of parents, kids, and dogs. In minutes all that was left in the lane leaving the parking lot were a cluster of bicycles and riders, Elise and her bags, and a Land Rover. Ahead, a magenta Lincoln Continental graced them all with a cloud of blue exhaust where it idled at the start of a paved two-lane road.

Elise approached the riders buckling on their helmets and swilling down Gatorade. "Can you tell me how far to a hotel, or a place for room and board?"

One of the spandex-clad riders looked up from the pack she was buckling onto her bike. "Ganges. Fourteen klicks."

Her jaw dropped. "Ganges is a town, I assume," she stammered.

The reply was a nod.

"Fourteen kilometres — *that* far?"

"A little shy of ten miles. You're not from around here?"

"I grew up in Ontario. I didn't think about Ganges being that far from the ferry," Elise said, feeling foolish. "Should have looked up the distance on the Internet. "

The bike riders headed away, one of them muttering, "Bloody tourists."

4

Ten miles! Fourteen klicks! Who would have figured that a small island off the coast of British Columbia would be big enough to have ten miles of road? She must have landed at the opposite end of Saltspring from this Ganges place. Maybe she would have been better off to try her rest cure back in Vancouver after all. "New places," she said under her breath. "I wanted to see new places. Well, I'm certainly going to see a lot of this new place, unless someone can tell me something about a bus or cab service." Angrily she thrust her arms through the straps on her knapsack and grabbed the duffle bag.

"Hello-oo," called a voice quietly. She didn't turn around.

Coasting up beside her as she left the parking lot came the Land Rover. "Hello again," called Dale through the open window. Something about the window was strange enough that she spared it a glance: half of the glass slid sideways behind a second pane, like a sliding door. Moss was growing in the window groove.

Elise kept walking.

"So you missed the bus. Or did your ride not turn up?" said Dale with a smile. "Were you stood up at the ferry terminal? Jilted at the dock by your long-awaited —"

"I didn't have a ride!" she admitted. "I had no idea what was here." She stopped next to the idling Lincoln. "Excuse me, do you know where a pay phone is?" she asked the grey haired man behind the wheel. Instead of answering, he rolled up his window and continued sorting papers into his briefcase. "Of all the... Did you see that?" she demanded of Dale, who had stopped beside her. "He won't even talk to me! Whatever happened to rural hospitality?" Meanwhile, the driver shifted his car into gear and drove away, engine building to a roar within a few moments.

Dale rested his chin on his fists, elbows on the Rover's wide steering wheel. "Nope. He especially won't talk to me, either. Not since I built him a rock garden behind that gallery of his and gave him an itemized bill for each rock."

In spite of herself, Elise giggled. Then she caught control again. "Where can I find a pay phone?"

"No cell phone?"

"I just use it on WIFI. No calls or texts. I can VOIP if there's free WIFI here..."

"Not till you get to Ganges, at the library and Mrs Blaus' deli." Dale shifted in the driver's seat, clasping hands behind his head. "There's a phone in the general store a block away. But it would be courtesy to buy ten dollars of groceries first, and tell Sunflower all about yourself, before asking to use the phone. All in all, it would take at least as long as walking a mile to the Fulford Inn and using the pay phone there. Can I give you a lift?"

"No, thanks. I'm calling a cab." Elise set off down the road. Only one road, she told herself. I can't go far wrong.

"Well, then, can I advertise the Willis Amateur Taxi Service?" His Land Rover was running at her side again. Dale opened the passenger door window, keeping one hand on the wheel and a frantic knee bumping the gear shift into second. "I'm trustworthy, thrifty, clean, loyal, and reverent. You'll never hear me blaspheme or make lewd comments."

"Bullshit," retorted Elise, shifting her duffle bag to the other hand. "What about fourteen GLORIOUS nights?" She kept walking.

"What about them?" He grinned, then saw her expression. "That wasn't lewd, that was suggestive. If you think that was lewd, you've got a dirty mind, Ms Hammell." The engine revved a little higher as he tapped the accelerator, but the Land Rover kept coasting.

He's got the clutch in, Elise realised. *Making noise like a high school kid with a hot old car. He should have outgrown that years ago — I haven't seen anyone do that since Scarborough Community School. All those shop jocks,* she remembered. *Proud of their expertise in car maintenance. Ha. Most of them could barely do an oil change.*

"Did you hear me, Ms Hammell? I said you've got a dirty mind," Dale called. She stopped dead in her tracks and slugged the door of the suddenly stationary Land Rover.

"Damn all you car shop wannabe fixers!" Elise caught her swinging duffle bag before it hit the fender. "Some day I'll learn how to do an oil change and then I'll be even with the lot of you." She stomped on along the road's gravel shoulder, past the general store, a small art gallery, an arts and crafts store, and an honest-to-god carrot juice stand.

Sixties refugees indeed. Looking at the carrot juice stand, Elise just couldn't hold on to her bad mood; she decided to enjoy the walk after all and see what she could of Fulford Harbour. Any place with a carrot juice stand couldn't be all bad. It might even be... interesting.

She was savouring the word — interesting — when the Land Rover came up cautiously from behind and kept pace with her as she walked. "Pardon me," called Dale with more meekness than she would have expected from him. "I seem to have blundered into an internal monologue. Let me introduce myself again. I am Dale Willis, of the Victoria Willises. I have lived here honourably for eight years since graduating from Camosun College and breaking my mother's heart by working with my hands. I have since broken my father's heart by every job that comes my way on this island, since none of them involve monopolies or dominating the market. I own my own mobile home, my Land Rover, and I am taking a course in French Cooking through University Extension." He drew a long breath and glanced at Elise to see if she was taking any of this in. "Twenty-seven years old, six foot one, no visible scars, brown eyes, black hair not going thin on top *yet*, thank God." He looked at her sidelong again. "Are you listening to any of this? I bare my past before you and you just take it in without comment."

"I hear you," said Elise, smiling.

They continued on in silence for another hundred of her steps.

"Well?" came the call again. "Have you no reply?"

She favoured him with a wink and kept walking.

"Come on. I told you mine. Now tell me yours."

Elise ran a thumb under a shoulder strap and shifted her knapsack. "Interesting? About my life? I came to Vancouver from Scarborough so I could go to university in a town that wasn't crammed full of my parents. Everywhere I went were their favourite restaurants, their friends' shops, the car salesman who sold them the Volvo. No room for my own memories." Walking like this proved to her that the hiking boots were a worthwhile investment. Imagine walking this road in sandals. "I've had four years of English Lit, re-reading books that I read on my own years ago and drawing conclusions that set *Coles' Notes* on its ear. Working every summer in Stanley Park. Boring. You want to know which year I read Joseph Conrad? I can't remember."

"Why aren't you at Stanley Park this summer?" A bee buzzed into the Land Rover. Dale chased it into the back seat.

"Because after graduation I sat down and read my roommate's comic book collection. She left them behind when she went to McGill to be a grad student. I spent five stupid weeks reading *Amethyst, Princess of Gemworld* and *Alpha Flight*." Elise shuddered. "When I finally realised I hadn't really eaten in a month, I sold her damned comic books and bought a fitness club membership to get back into shape."

"You're still skinny," Dale called, ducking the bee as it came past his ear. It buzzed out the window and into a patch of fireweed beside the road.

"Thank you, Alex Trebec. I'm no candidate for Miss Universe. Neither were the people in the fitness club. A bunch of uncommunicative idiots always looking at themselves in the mirror." Elise polished a scuff off the top of her boot and continued walking. "Fitness club gave me a refund real fast after I fainted during a workout. 'Don't push so hard,' they told me. 'Find something that interests you without killing you.' I've sort of taken it as my motto."

"Find something that interests you without killing you," said Dale, drawing out the words. "I've heard worse mottoes. What are you going to find here?"

"Beats me. You're the local, you tell me. I'm just a bloody tourist. What about the thriving art community on Saltspring?" Elise could see the Fulford Inn looming up.

"Ah yes, the thriving art community. I take it you have had a surfeit of writers during the last few years..." intoned Dale through his nose. "Let me recommend instead the art galleries of the island. We have galleries of many persuasions: the macrame and tie-dye school of interior decorating, the oil painting in gilded frame gallery where you don't dare wipe your feet on their door mat, the souvenir store thinly disguised as a classy gallery... oh, the list goes on. Ah ha! You're giggling again. I like that. I prescribe it. One giggle every ten minutes until no pain is felt."

"I wasn't giggling," Elise protested.

"A chuckle then. Nothing like the silly snigger of adolescent girls."

"I give up. You're irrepressible. You're going to shower me with all these comments until..." Elise let the words trail away.

"Until what?" Dale glanced at her, then back to the road.

"Until I spill the real reason I came to Saltspring."

"So spill it. But for heaven's sake, wait til I park this beast." Dale turned the Land Rover into the parking lot of the Fulford Inn, and found a place near the pay phone. "Now spill it. I'm all ears."

"It's petroglyphs." Elise was suddenly embarrassed. "I heard there were petroglyphs on Saltspring and so I came here instead of just anywhere."

"You gotta be kidding." Dale swung his door open and turned the motor off. "What's a college girl got to interest her in a bunch of rocks instead of books?"

"I saw one. It got to me. After all this contact with so-called sophisticated literature and art forms you're supposed to study for four years just to appreciate, let alone create, it... got to me. It was real art."

Elise looked at her feet. "One of my professors had one in his living room. He told me a little about them, and the First Nations people who carved them."

Dale moved to touch her arm, and she looked up. "You said someone you know has one in his living room? That's illegal as anything. They're considered historical objects of the First Nations who live near the stone. Property of the band council, or the federal government, or something. Not something other people can take home and put in their living rooms."

"I don't know how he got it. He just told me that there were some petroglyphs on Saltspring Island, and other places around the Coast. Now if you'll pardon me, I have a call to make." Elise had spied the pay phone, and went to make her call. Dale waited, and the motor ticked as it cooled.

In a minute she was back. "You have a very brief Yellow Pages section in your phone book, do you know that?" She dumped the duffle bag at her feet and faced Dale. "I got an answering machine that says SS Cabs will not be picking up passengers today as Harry's daughter is having a baby and Harry is waiting at the hospital for word. It also said all bets are closed for the baby pool."

"Let's hear it for luck," Dale crowed. "Today is my day for the pool. I hope she has that baby before midnight."

"Now how am I going to get to Ganges?"

Dale tucked his thumbs behind his brass belt buckle and grinned. "Want to go for a ride, little girl?"

"I guess I don't have much choice. Are you going to give me more of this chatter and suggestive talk?" asked Elise as she picked up her duffle bag.

Dale slung the duffle into the back seat and took her knapsack to do the same. "I will speak only when spoken to. It's my day off, and you're more fun to talk to than the raccoon living under my deck. You don't trust me yet? We'll have to go to the deli and get Mrs Blaus to give you a character reference for me. Then you'll trust me."

"Not bloody likely," muttered Elise. She walked behind the Land Rover and over to the passenger door as Dale opened it from inside. "What sort of a beast is a Land Rover, anyways?"

"It is the British answer to the jeep, designed for use in the desert fighting Rommel's army," Dale replied in a crisp British accent. "At five miles an hour, pardon me, eight kilometres an hour, it is possible to crank the wheel hard over and slowly, with complete control, turn this beast onto its back." Dale paused and let the accent lapse. "Turning it back onto its wheels is another matter entirely. At any rate, I've got my eye on an electric car for when this beast finally gives up the ghost."

"It's certainly different." Elise hunted for her seat belt buckle. "I'd call it unique."

"It's the only beige four-seater on the island," said Dale proudly. "There's a couple of green two-seaters in Vesuvius. Now, where to? A hotel, bed-and-breakfast, or would you like to see a petroglyph?" He gestured in the direction of the sun, which was just clearing the bulk of the mountain they'd seen from the ferry.

"What, now?" Elise turned the rear-view mirror in her direction and combed her hair with her fingers before turning the mirror back more-or-less where it had been. "Is it far? I'd like to rent a room before noon." *As if I have plans for more than walking around*, she admitted to herself.

"You've just walked farther," Dale assured her as he put the Rover in gear and backed it out of the parking spot. He turned onto the road and tore past an intersection without slowing down. "Stay cool," he advised her. "I had the right-of-way. Island residents carrying tourist passengers have the right-of-way over residents or tourists. It's in the bylaws. But really, the fields on either side of that intersection mean I could see for a mile along both roads. No traffic, not even a cat crossing the road."

"Thank heaven for small mercies," groaned Elise, gripping her car seat with both hands. The lurch of the next turn nearly unseated her. "Drive with Dale Willis and learn all about acceleration. I should have waited for SS Cabs." The next turn sent her duffle bag to the floor, and she scrabbled for it, checking for breakage, muttering to herself. "What does SS Cabs stand for — Salt Spring?"

"Well, maybe it did at first." Dale shook his head. "But somebody decided it must stand for the German SS that Harry's dad worked in during the war. Harry even joined the Royal Canadian Legion, as a veteran's family member."

"But he was in the wrong army!"

"Hey, the Chamber of Commerce held a big consultation with locals who lost family during the war. Called in a rep from the Legion, the high school History teacher, and a First Nations elder. They looked at Harry's logo & lettering and listened to his story, asked him about his life and work." Dale guided the Rover around another curve. "It helped that Harry's family never lied about his dad's war service. And they're part of Orange Shirt Day and Remembrance Day events."

Once again, Elise found herself unable to hold on to her disbelief. Any place with a German soldier's offspring in the Legion had to be... interesting. Now if it only had good roads! She said as much out loud.

"This is not one of our better roads," he admitted. He gestured at the fields and scrubby apple trees they were passing on one side of the road. "There's only a couple of farms along the inlet here, so the road was minimally graded before paving. It's lasted well for years as far as the surface goes. What you're complaining about," and he brought the Land Rover into a small cul-de-sac that overlooked the harbour, "is the roller-coaster effect we get because this adequate surface was laid on an uneven bed. And we're here."

"Here?" All Elise could see was more of Fulford Harbour, the inlet, which they'd been driving along. Fulford Harbour, the hamlet, was across the inlet: a bright little collection of houses, shops and three churches in a line from a hillside to the water's edge.

"Drummond Park. Scene of barbecues, picnics, late afternoon swims when the incoming tide is warmed by the sun-baked sand." Dale gestured with his hands wide. "And, one certified authentic petroglyph. With a plaque to identify it, which is lucky for you. Most of the other carved rocks are on beaches crammed with other rocks and you have to be shown where to look." He raised an eyebrow. "Shall we take a look?"

Elise nodded and fumbled with the door latch. Once she figured the method, the door opened easily. She slipped out and joined Dale under three red cedar trees near the edge of the sand. "How old are the trees?" she asked, one hand on the rough bark, one clutching her duffle bag.

"Oh, these are little ones. Maybe a hundred years old. Most of the island was logged off around a hundred years ago and what you'll see by the road is new growth." Dale patted a large, egg-shaped rock. "Are you still interested?"

"This is it?" With a small thrill of delight, Elise stroked the rock. Shallow grooves marked the upper surface of the stone, which was nearly flat and at waist height on her. "It's much bigger than the other one I saw. What's the design? Oh, I see — a face with round eyes and a, a smile?" Suddenly she smiled too, and felt her face soften, as if it had been growing stiff. "It's not very easy to see, but if I make a rubbing of it then the pattern will be clear." She took a roll of coarse paper and a black-coloured pad from her duffle bag.

Dale watched with some interest as she taped the paper in place and brushed the pad over the coarse sheet. The round-eyed face was visible in a few strokes, and became clearer as she learned how to handle the pad. "Not bad," he said approvingly. "Now what do you do with it?"

"I store it rolled in this tube until I can hang it on a wall or press it into a scrapbook," Elise informed him. "This is the first of a collection. I guess I'd like to make a rubbing of every petroglyph I find while I'm here." She scribbled the date and *Drummond Park, Fulford Harbour* on the rolled paper, then dropped the pencil and paper inside a sturdy mailing tube in her duffle bag.

"And now to Ganges?" he asked. "There'll be time to find you a hotel and have a meal by noon. Hungry?" They turned back towards his vehicle and this time she passed in front of it.

"What's this for?" She pointed at some contraption on the front bumper. Dale didn't even glance at it, just got behind the wheel as he spoke.

"That's a winch. Not all Rovers have them. If you're driving off-road and want to go up a really steep incline, that gets you up there." He turned a CB radio on briefly, to hear the static crackle, then off. When Elise had settled herself and her gear in the passenger seat, Dale started the engine and put them back on the road again. "You anchor a steel cable to something solid at the top, and let the winch pull the car uphill. I don't get much chance to drive off-road on Saltspring. Most of the land is owned by very possessive people who put barbed-wire fences and machine gun nests around their property." He glance over to see if she was still listening. "I lied about the machine gun nests," he added.

Looking out the window, Elise watched the farms go by: apple trees, a few sheep or goats, once a big market garden. "I'm learning to tell when you're lying," she told him dryly. "But I'm still not sure about SS Cabs."

"That is gospel truth," Dale said firmly. "You'll learn one thing about me. I never interfere with the truth when anyone can check up on me. I become creative with my stories only when I'm given a free rein to tell them."

They were rumbling along a straight stretch of road when she thought to ask Dale how fast a Land Rover could go. Instantly she regretted the impulse, assuming that he would simply demonstrate. To her surprise, he continued past a sheep pasture and thickly forested woodlot at a steady eighty klicks. "I don't know," he admitted. "I've never really opened 'er up and found out. This is the longest bit of straight road we've got, and it's already been speed-tested by that monster of a purple Lincoln Continental you saw this morning."

"I thought it was magenta," Elise answered. "The colour of a bad cigar. The colour of a mafia don's tie. The colour of a bruise."

"It's easy to tell you studied great works in literature. You have such a way with words, a knack for description that almost matches mine." They had begun to enter a more thickly populated area; new houses were going up between older ones and perhaps one in four were for sale. "Now me, *my* higher education has been considerably assisted by compulsive watching of Monty Python skits."

For the rest of the journey into town he sang "I'm a lumberjack and I'm okay" until she was ready to get out and walk.

When he parked in front of the docks in Ganges and pointed out a hotel, Elise grabbed both her bags. "Well, so long, Dale, and thanks for the ride," she said brightly. "It's been real, and it's been fun, but it hasn't been real fun. See you around." She swept out of the car and walked quickly across the road and into the hotel.

Two minutes later, she walked just as quickly out of it. How could they charge that much a night?! That's what she got for coming here during the summer season, like a tourist. And she had no camping gear for an alternative. Maybe she'd be better off trying to rent a furnished room for a few weeks. A hotel room would eat up the bankroll from the sale of her roommate's comic book collection in a a matter of days.

Next door was a real estate office and property management firm. Pay dirt! In twenty minutes she'd picked not a furnished room but a small one-bedroom house on the Fulford Ganges Road, paid the deposit and a month's rent, filled out forms and been assured of a refund of a week or more's worth of rent if she decided to leave early. The old fellow behind the counter had been most helpful and given her his card. *Jim Wickers*, she read.

"My home phone number is on the card as well as my business number, Ms Hammell. You can call me if you have any trouble with the house at all," said Wickers. "Or call my wife and ask her to tell you where to find things. She's a finder, that's what she is."

"Can you find something for me right now, Mr Wickers?" Elise asked. "I'm starving. Someplace quick, nearby, and cheap?"

"Anywhere on the block will do for quick and nearby," Wickers told her, and polished his glasses. He settled his thick and compact body into his wooden desk chair. "But if you take my advice, you'll walk to the left until you smell pizza." He set his hands on the oak arms of his captain's chair, worn and stained from years of use.

She thanked him and left the office with a bit more energy in her step. Pizza! Now why couldn't she remember how much she liked pizza, when she was bored and looking for something to do? Having pizza for her was almost on the order of a party in itself, something that lifted her out of any brooding to concentrate solely on taste and texture and smell. She saw the sign for the pizza place and her mouth watered. Home-made sauce, eh? This looked like something good was about to happen.

At the back table out of five was a familiar figure: Dale, with a large pepperoni pizza in front of him, and only one piece eaten.

With a flush, she remembered her cavalier leave-taking. She hadn't needed to be so abrupt. It had been less than an insult, but not by much.

Just then, Dale looked up from the pizza and spied her at the door. To her shame, he waved her over immediately, and moved the pizza so that it was centred between the table's two chairs. She came up hesitantly and spoke to him.

"I'm kind of embarrassed —"

"Forget it." Dale waved a piece of pepperoni-covered heaven at her. She sniffed greedily. "If I took offence at things like that, I'd have to ignore half the world. Matter of fact, I've just been remembering twenty-seven choruses of 'I'm a lumberjack' and I'm kind of embarrassed, too."

"Don't say them." Elise gritted her teeth. She slipped into the chair and took the wedge of pizza from his hand. "Don't even think about that song or I will not eat this — hmmm — exshellent pizzsha with you," she lisped, then paused to chew and swallow. "I've rented a place. Somewhere along the road we came in on. It's small but looks like a cute little cabin."

"Good," said Dale casually. "Here's a map of Saltspring for you. Where's the place?"

"The property manager said it was where Lee Road joined the highway. Imagine calling that road a highway," Elise mumbled the last part around a mouthful of home-made sauce and crust. She spread the map out on the table and forever afterwards in her mind's eye, Ruckle Park would be identified by a large grease stain. "Oh, for Pete's sake. I'm in the same predicament I was this morning. At least this time it's only an eight kilometre walk."

"I don't think you've really got the scale of the island yet," Dale said with a smile. "Can I take you around it and show you some of the best places?"

"As long as Harry, son of an SS veteran, is waiting for his daughter to have the baby, I guess I haven't much choice." Elise took another piece of pizza and concentrated on the oregano in the sauce.

"There's a bus every two hours between Fulford and Ganges," Dale began, then smacked the table with the flat of his hand. Oval, rounded fingernails, she noted, and was surprised at herself. Previously she had only been able to notice pizza while eating one that was this well-prepared. "You reminded me! *Keefer,*" he called to the man behind the counter. Elise winced at the volume but since everyone in the tiny pizza place was talking nearly as loudly themselves, no one took any notice but Keefer himself. "Get over here, you old hippie, and tell me if I won the baby pool."

"I'm working, man, leave me alone," came a reply. "Nobody's won the pool yet. I'm getting progress reports from Harry every hour. You'll have to wait like everyone else. Babies come when they come."

Dale shrugged and devoted himself to another piece of pizza. "I guess that's that for now. Personally, when I want to do something, I just get down and do it. No —" He paused to remove a string of mozzarella cheese from his chin. "No fiddling around with maybe next week. I'd never have gotten the wiring done in the mobile home with an attitude like that."

"Maybe that's why you can't give birth." Elise put the crust in her mouth and reached for the last piece. "I pity any wife of yours, getting told when and how to have your baby. But what's that got to do with wiring your mobile home?"

"The electrician I called was booked up solid, he thought, for the next six weeks when I needed the place set up as soon as possible. So I signed up for an electrician's course through University Extension and learned how to do it from the textbooks. The inspector came by and told me it was up to scratch, so I finished the entire program and got my ticket. I do about three houses a year, now, could be more if I wanted to get cracking." Dale paused, and went to the counter to pick up a couple of Cokes. "Talking and pizza are a lethal combination on the throat. Have a Coke?"

"It's not the diet stuff, is it?" Elise was wary of diet soda pop. She'd heard enough about aspartame to keep her from ever drinking diet again.

"Nope. Only the classic here in the Pizza Closet." Dale downed half his drink in one gulp. "Anyways, this attitude of getting things done right now if you want them done, I admire that in you. 'Find something that interests you without killing you,' and, sonufagun, you do it. Petroglyphs. Then you actually take a friend's advice and go where there are some."

"Not a friend," Elise admitted. "A professor. I actually don't like him much; he reminds me of the man in the Lincoln Continental this morning. Who is he, Dale? You said something about building a rock garden behind his art gallery."

"Oh, *that*." Dale finished his drink, then spoke at a quieter volume than he had been. "The Sunset Gallery is run by J. Vaughn Laging, who is as Anglo-Saxon as you but has a Dutch great-grandfather. He puts the letters "UE" behind his name to advertise that he is also descended from a United Empire Loyalist, but I think he takes after the Dutch side more. I've never seen anyone stretch an income so far."

"How far is far?" Elise drank her Coke, enjoying the bite of it as she had the oregano tang in the sauce. Nothing like a Coke on a warm day. Not after a pizza. Things were looking better already. Damn near interesting.

"Far is keeping that Lincoln on the road in spite of the way he drives it, and keeping all of his property on Saint Mary Lake when anyone else would have subdivided it by now. It's mostly wooded, with trails running through a couple of acres, then gardens and the house and gallery up by the road. When I built that rock garden I cemented a bunch together and set several loose ones around the cluster. He didn't want any flowers in it at all, said he had enough rose bushes. J. Vaughn Laging wanted rocks, so I prepared the space and gave him two dozen beauties that nearly broke my back and my winch moving them around. He didn't like my itemized bill listing each rock, and he paid me in cash."

"That's a problem?" Elise raised eyebrows till they disappeared under her bangs. "I thought a handyman and jack-of-all-trades would prefer cash."

"Every try to deposit nine hundred and ninety two one-dollar coins? Loose, not rolled?" Dale asked sourly. "The bank tellers had a fun time with them, let me tell you. 'Oh, Doris, we'd better check them. He might have a counterfeiting machine rigged up out in his workshop.'" He grimaced. "Come on, let's head over to your new place and then out to see another petroglyph. Or an art gallery."

"No singing," warned Elise as she got up. "I want to spend this trip enjoying the scenery, not hanging my head out the window and throwing up all this pizza."

"Whatsamatta, ya don't like my singing?" Dale led the way to his Land Rover.

"I don't like the song. Plus anything twenty times in a row is too much." Elise put her gear in the back and opened the map again. Once buckled in, she spread it over her lap and cheerfully ignored Dale's whistling of Roger Whittaker's greatest hits.

She looked up at intervals, following their route on the map until the car stopped. Then to her delight, Elise found that they were in front of a small brown and white house with a fenced yard, surrounded on three sides by the sheep pasture she had seen earlier. "This is mine?" To the student who'd been sharing a tiny apartment in downtown Vancouver for four years, it was like a fantasy. There were even five sheep grazing close by the fence. Maybe, she wondered, there were more sheep in a barn on the far side of the little rise where the house was built.

"I'll wait here," Dale said, resigned to waiting. "Check it out and come out when you're ready." He pulled the January 2002 edition of *Fantasy and Science Fiction* magazine out of the glove compartment.

"Isn't that magazine a little out of date?"

"I'm a collector," he said brusquely. "Go. Explore."

She was back in fifteen minutes. "There are windows *everywhere*," were her first words. "And a Franklin stove in the living room, a little wood-burning stove instead of a fireplace. I've made the bed and sat in all the chairs. From the back windows all I can see is pasture, sky and trees. I'm going to like it here," she finished as she clambered into the Land Rover, a nearly empty duffle bag in her hand. "At least, it would take an awful lot to keep me from liking it. All right, Dale. Let's go to a gallery and then shop for some food for my fridge. And let me buy some gas to thank you for all this driving."

They went through a handful of small galleries in Ganges, that had clever clay mugs with faces carved into them, and macrame wall hangings that could cover entire walls, and small sculptural human figures twisted out of copper wire. One souvenir store had an oven in a back room, sending out the most delectable smell of oatmeal chocolate chip cookies. On the way to the grocery store afterwards, Dale pulled in to a service station just as J. Vaughn Laging drove up to the other side of the pump.

The pump jockey came out, was waved on by Dale, and headed for the big Lincoln. A window rolled down and a grey head was visible within. "Fill it up. And check the oil, the brakes, and the shocks," Laging said curtly. The attendant nodded, and set about all these things.

Getting Dale to accept some money towards gas took persuasion, but Elise insisted. After, she fidgeted until they had been serviced as well, taking time to read signs on the gas station wall saying "Full Service" "Fast Charge for Electric Cars" and "E-Bike Rentals." As they left, the pump jockey called a goodbye to Dale by name. "Do you know everybody on this island?"

"Nope," said Dale cheerfully. "But I know who knows whom, and who does what, and who can find what. I've worked with almost all the trades people round here, and done work for all the people with big money."

"Do you know Mrs Wickers?"

"She's a fine lady." He parked in front of the grocery. "This is where she buys her food. I trust her judgment enough to get my stuff here, too, or at the farmers' market on Saturdays."

It came to mind that she was trusting his judgment a great deal. She'd driven and walked about with him most of the day, now, and still had little idea of how he usually spent his time. Or where he lived. She began to brood on these thoughts while selecting groceries and paying for them. *Eggs, milk — and what's his last name again? Willis, right. — Bread, peanut butter, tea — I'm being paranoid. No one's so much as looked sideways at him after saying hello. They treat him as if he's what he says he is: some sort of fixit man who's worked for everyone.*

I have to trust someone, she realised, and felt the tight knot in her stomach disappear as they carried a grocery bag each out to the Land Rover. *I needed someone today who'll do what he's doing, especially if Harry the cab driver is taking time off. I'll have to trust him to some extent and see if I can get to know him.*

Now if only I can keep him from singing the same song over and over, thought Elise. The Rover rumbled quietly as it carried them back to her house. Engrossed with her thoughts, she played with the moss in the window groove and said nothing for a few minutes.

Dale cleared his throat. "I've got plans for tonight, so if it's all the same to you, Elise, I'll just drop you off now and come by in the morning to show you some petroglyphs on a beach. How's nine o'clock sound to you?"

"Oh, sure, nine o'clock's okay." Had he known that would give her such a sense of relief, not to feel obliged to invite him in? She had her doubts whether the plans for tonight involved anything more pre-arranged than, say, working on a model airplane. She wasn't asking questions. Let him be noble. It was easier that way.

With real gratitude she said good night after wrestling the bag of groceries and her duffle bag onto the porch. No sticky goodbyes at the door from him; he'd waved from the car. But also, no assistance with the groceries. Obviously he was not to be taken for granted. *So what, that's fine. All the best men are either already married or gay*, Elise reminded herself. It was one of the cardinal laws of the universe.

Time for an omelette, she decided, and set about assembling a marvellous omelette to eat sitting cross-legged on the small deck behind the house. Sheep were walking lazily near the fence as the sun set, and a fat raccoon waddled out from under the deck without so much as a glance in her direction. The whole scene was so pastoral that Elise felt she just had to do something to maintain the mood as it got dark. She ended up curled in bed reading *The Life of Saint Francis of Assisi*. It was, she decided, considerably more difficult than reading *Amethyst, Princess of Gemworld*. There was no way to understand why her roommate had left the biography behind with all her comic books.

At 12:30 she awoke abruptly to the sound of a powerful car engine. It came from the direction of Ganges, roaring down the hill, gears shifting audibly as it passed and rounded a bend. Lying in bed, she heard the car continue on, revving loud and hard, the sound carrying over the fields mixed with a few bleats from startled sheep. Her heart raced until she realised that it probably wasn't the volunteer fire fighters out on a call. *Nothing as sinister as even that*, she told herself. *It's probably Laging out road-racing that big old Lincoln of his. Dale said that this stretch of road had been speed-tested, remember?* With that, she smiled away the last of the shivers and settled back to sleep.

An hour later the car, now on its return journey, woke her again and she blackly cursed J. Vaughn Laging or whoever was driving. She listened to it pass with the sound of a strong man's anger, or a dog's trained growl. One curl of the lip, no more. It was harder to sleep again this time.

AT 9:05 THE NEXT MORNING, Dale honked the horn for her. When she threw her duffle bag in the back, it landed next to a picnic basket.

"Somebody's been thinking ahead!" This day might be shaping up fine, Elise decided.

"Not so far ahead as might be. That basket is only half full," Dale admitted as they set out. "We'll stop at the deli in Ganges and stock up."

"Liverwurst. If they have liverwurst, all will be right with the world." She settled back to enthuse about liverwurst until Dale was almost in the state she had been the day before during his singing. She graciously ceased her ode to the joys of liverwurst as they entered the deli, picnic basket in one of Dale's broad hands.

"Morning, Mrs Blaus. Could you give a character reference for me to my date?" Dale began taking packages from the shelves and dumping them in Elise's arms. "Mrs Blaus, meet Elise Hammell."

"He is a bit overwhelming at times." Mrs Blaus smiled. One of her eyes had a cataract or something, Elise guessed, but her gaze was steady and direct. "I've known him for years, ever since his folks bought some properties on Saltspring. He takes my grandchildren swimming when they come to visit." She smoothed the apron at her thick waist and cut thin slices from a Gouda cheese for Dale.

"So he's trustworthy with small children." Elise laughed. "Trustworthy, thrifty, clean, loyal, and reverent. Sounds like a real Boy Scout." When Dale asked in a whisper if she had any allergies, she shook her head, no.

"Oh yes, he's handy as any Boy Scout," agreed Mrs Blaus, wrapping the cheese. She set it in a bag with the liverwurst and other packages. "I do wish he'd stick to one career, though. It's one thing to learn all that you do, Dale, but when are you going to start putting a little aside for your future? And when are you going to build that house you were talking about?"

"When I get around to it," Dale mumbled around a fresh rye bun he'd pulled from the bag. "The workshops were more important first. You know that."

"And then the extension courses were more important. I don't think you'll really have a reason to build a real house for yourself until you settle down and get married." Mrs Blaus rang up the bill on her register.

"I bet you say that to all your customers." Dale accepted half the cost from Elise and paid the bill. "That, my dear surrogate grandma, is why I am known as One-Date Dale around here. Two dates with me and you've linked our names forever in the mouths of town gossips."

"Get out with you, now." The older woman turned her gaze, bright green eye and dimmed blue eye, on Elise. "Where are you going today?"

"Off to see petroglyphs and art galleries," replied Elise.

"Get him to drop you off at the Sunset Gallery, then," advised Mrs Blaus. "My husband says they've got another new showing of those petroglyph rubbings. No sense missing it just because Dale and Mr Laging don't get along."

"I wouldn't dream of it," Elise said with a smile. *That bad, eh?*

Dale finished packing the new supplies into the picnic basket. Elise caught a glimpse of a bottle of wine, and one of Coke as he closed the lid. "Let's be off while the tide is still going out. See you soon," he called back as he left with Elise in tow.

"That was more than slightly embarrassing," he said finally, when they were rocketing down a road she hadn't seen before, considerably faster than yesterday's conservative speed.

"Oh, I don't know," answered Elise. "I found it pretty informative, One-Date. Tell me, since this is our second day in company, does that link us forever in the mouths of town gossips?"

"Only if Mrs Blaus hears about it," Dale growled, and backed off on the accelerator. They took a corner and wobbled a bit, but all four wheels settled back on the ground. "Never fear, this Rover's got a roll bar. Care to do a little four-wheel driving?"

"You drive," she gasped as the road climbed sharply and the sound of the engine changed under his control. "I'll cling. Why did I ever eat breakfast?"

They passed a few isolated houses set well back from the road, under arbutus trees. "Architect's nightmares, all of them," Dale snorted. Instead of pine and fir trees along this road, there were mostly arbutus and oak trees. Dry curls of shredded bark lined the roadside or scudded rustily in front of the Land Rover.

"Who lives along here?" asked Elise, getting a figurative grip on her stomach.

"Rich people with summer houses. When you don't see a house for a while, that means someone bought the land and plans to subdivide it for a profit in a few years." Dale kicked the engine down a gear and gripped the wheel more tightly. "A friend of mine has some waterfront land we'll use to access a beach with a couple of petroglyphs."

"How many are there?" The flutter in Elise's stomach turned to excitement.

"No one ever knows how many petroglyphs there ARE at any one place. All you know is how many you've FOUND. Sometimes you find one when moss gets stripped off a half-ton boulder or some bedrock. Sometimes you look on the lower curve of a rock that's only exposed by low tide. And sometimes they're only visible when the light is at the right angle." Back in third gear, the engine sounded more like its usual purring self. "I've found three at this beach. One is only visible at low tide. Can you imagine whoever carved it, lying on the wet stones for an hour or so at a time?"

"I wonder how long it took to carve," she mused.

Dale pulled the Land Rover to a stop as they came down to the bottom of a hill. Seawater glinted ahead, past bushes and beached logs. "Near as I can figure, time isn't important in the same way for First Nations people, and even more so back then. What was more important was what they were doing. Some of these carvings are religious artifacts, and it was an act of worship to make them. If I understand it right," he admitted. "A few of the designs commemorate important events."

"And the rest?"

"Kilroy was here. Grab your duffle and we'll go find some pre-colonial graffiti."

Elise tugged on the bushes as they passed. "I know what this plant is. My roommate Lyn called it salal. Why's it so tall, though?"

"Natural habitat. Wait till you get away from a road. Try to follow a stream and you'll find salal bushes growing taller than you." Dale stepped over a weather-silvered log, swinging the picnic basket as if it were much lighter than Elise knew it to be.

Several hundred yards down the beach a small point of land jutted out into the waves. They clambered across this point, slipping on wet grass and clay. "Why is it wet?" asked Elise. "It hasn't been raining today."

"Under the trees like this, downhill from that hill we drove down, the ground can stay damp. Clay always feels damp to me anyway." Dale wiped a blue-grey smear on his jeans. *He was wearing the belt again,* Elise noticed. *The one with the ornate brass belt buckle. Where'd he get it?* she wondered, then put it out of her mind as he helped her clamber down onto the rocky sand. He pointed out a small boulder.

It was that warm feeling she'd had on seeing the carrot juice stand, all over again. She felt her smile grow, and saw Dale's answering smile. Making her second, third, and fourth petroglyph rubbing was just as pleasing as the first had been. This new activity actually was interesting, Elise realised with some relief. Four years of study at university to get recognition for what she already knew had given her a keen appreciation of the new.

And she couldn't call this hobby hokey or mind-candy after lying on wet rocks to finish working on a carving that the tide would soon cover. She didn't feel like some half-hearted collector of lazy art forms. She felt almost like she belonged on a rocky island beach with a jack-of-all-trades pouring Mateus wine into a silver goblet for her.

"Silver! Just how rich are the Victoria Willises?" She drank the rose wine in a gulp. The salt air had made her thirsty.

"Not rich enough to afford new glasses for every picnic," was Dale's reply. "I got one of these goblets as a high school grad present and another on finishing at Fairy Tech. Rather than leave them to tarnish in my mother's china cabinets, I use them on picnics and get them honourably dinged up. More wine?"

Elise shook her head and combed through her bangs with her fingers. "Better make this one soda pop until I see how the wine gets to me."

"Suit yourself." Dale poured his own and corked the bottle "I'll keep to one glass myself as I'm driving. When it's your turn to drive sometime, then watch out! And you can pour me into the back seat with a spoon."

"You drink like that?" Having found the liverwurst, Elise made a couple of sandwiches.

"Only when I can find someone I trust to drive the Rover home." Dale worked on a Dagwood sandwich for himself. The rye bun held multiple layers of Gouda and Edam cheeses with lots of liverwurst, generously daubed with mustard.

"This goblet IS pretty dinged up," Elise commented as she filled it with pop. "Many picnics, Mr One-Date?"

"Jealous, Ms Hammell-with-the-dirty-mind?" He devoted some time to his sandwich before speaking again. "Lay off with the speculation, eh? Mrs Blaus and Sunflower at the general store took over that department when I moved here year-round instead of just summers."

She managed to keep the conversation to the "pass the mustard" level after that comment. When the food was gone, Dale showed her how to find pools of seawater along the shore as the tide slowly crept in. He had names for every kind of animal in the tide pools. A green sea anemone sucked on the end of Elise's finger, after he assured her the small beast was not poisonous.

"It feels like chewing gum," she said, and laughed.

"*There's* that chuckle again. Remember your prescription."

"I'm feeling no pain," Elise pointed out.

Dale sketched a mark in the air on his imaginary blackboard. "That's two. Watch it woman, you're getting close."

Abruptly Elise's smile faltered. She rolled her sleeves back down and tucked in the tail of her plaid shirt. "Weren't we going to a gallery this afternoon?"

Dale backed away with a frown between his eyes, but he picked up the picnic basket without complaint. "Sure, but let's not make it the Sunset Gallery. "You've already got rubbings of three of his stones."

"What, *these*? J. Vaughn Laging owns this beach?" The idea had never occurred to her. "People can *own* beaches? Beaches are just there, like the ocean, or clouds."

"Just down to the high tide line. And lucky for us, all three of these stones are just slightly below that mark." Dale helped her up and across the point again. "It took a year, moving those rocks an inch at a time and no more often than once a week, but the two that were originally on his part of the beach are now on Crown land, the area below the high tide mark."

"Wow." She pondered his sneaky action. "You got the carvings out of his control. Way to go!"

"Actually, I have no idea whether or not Laging knew anything about the petroglyphs at all," he admitted. "It just pissed me off to see them on his land. He doesn't even live here. This lot is some investment for his retirement if the gallery business stops being so profitable."

"Oh. Do you ever do anything from a sense of noble purpose, or dull things like law and order?" Elise was a little ashamed of the gosh-wow admiring glance she had thrown him.

"I always check out the facts." Dale swung the basket into the back seat of the Land Rover. "I have to be ready in case someone checks up on my story." He made a move as if to tweak her nose. "Got to be above reproach, y'know."

"Don't pinch my nose!" she barked. It really was a bark, she realised: short, sharp and harsh. "Don't try to play with me like a little girl."

"Look, what do you want, an apology? You flirt a little and then clam up. Scared you'll enjoy it?" A muscle rippled beside Dale's jaw. "So you get a little teasing and an affectionate gesture and then *whammo*! You blow up. Will you for heaven's sake loosen up? I am not about to rape you. Or give you a lollipop."

"I've had enough time in your company," snapped Elise. "I don't want to hear any more of this. I'm walking back to Ganges."

"Oh, great God in heaven, look down on woman and repent that you have made her irritable." When it came to arguing, Dale had the techniques down pat. That rolling of the eyes now; funny how when she was bristling mad she could still take note of his good dramatic performance. It didn't matter, though. Elise had seen enough.

She started up the long hill, duffle bag across her shoulder.

"Hey!" The deep voice drifted up the road. "Take all the right hand forks where roads meet and you'll find your way." Elise didn't turn around. "Thank you VERY MUCH YOURSELF!" Dale worked himself up to a roar. "See if I waste gas following along beside you this time!"

In a minute he had the Land Rover started and heading up the hill past her. He didn't spray Elise with gravel. No, that wouldn't be like him, she realised, wiping at her hot cheeks. Instead he revved the engine with the clutch in again, like he had before she slugged the door. Like a kid in Auto Mechanics 12. Just to bug her.

She found a rock and threw it but missed the rear window. *So what.* Elise trudged along to the top of the hill. *Every right fork, eh?* It only took her an hour and a quarter to get back to Ganges. Luckily she'd worn her hiking boots.

There was a fine film of dust over Elise's entire body when she finally trudged into what was arguably Ganges village proper, not just a few scattered houses along the road. She had a blister on one heel and a raging thirst. As well, she was seriously contemplating putting Dale Willis and J. Vaughn Laging together in that big magenta sedan and sending them both off a cliff into the ocean at one o'clock in the morning. Waiting at the corner of Rainbow Road was a clean white cab with a pride rainbow bumper sticker, and a white-haired man leaning against it.

"Would you be Harry of SS Cabs?" Elise asked wearily.

"That's me."

"Are you accepting fares now?"

"I'll take you. Where you going?"

She gave him the address and slid into the front passenger seat when he opened the door. Thank goodness for small mercies. The cab was cool and smelled faintly but pleasantly of Harry's wintergreen gum.

"How's your daughter?" Elise could feel the coolness clearing her head.

Harry started the car and its electric motor hummed almost silently. "She's fine. She just had a little girl last night. Doctor says she can come home tomorrow."

"You didn't turn on the meter," observed Elise. The old fellow certainly didn't *look* senile by any standards she knew, she thought.

"Don't need to. Fella who won the baby pool paid me for the rest of the day. 'Harry,' he says, 'you'll see a pretty girl come along here in a minute. A skinny one with hair blowing all over and probably a real mad look on her face, but she's real pretty, Harry.'" The cab stopped for the village's one traffic light. "Then he tells me to take you wherever you want for the rest of the day and evening but, if you want, he says there's an apology and a proper bottle of wine waiting at La Firenze restaurant at seven o'clock."

Harry rounded the corner. "Then he gave me some money, so don't worry about the taxi meter. You know, I like driving cab a lot better than my old job in the mill. They made me retire at sixty-five. I've been driving cab for ten years, never an accident yet, knock on wood, and now I get a day like this. Life's not so bad for an old man, you know. I never thought I'd be married or have a family but I did, and I never thought I'd live to be seventy-five and hold my little granddaughter. Or help a friend make an apology like this." He looked over at his passenger.

Elise was slumped back in her seat, shaking helplessly with laughter. "Life is just one damn carrot juice stand after another!" she choked at last. "Why should I ever be crabby? Pull into that service station for a minute, please, Harry."

The attendant came over and she rolled down the window. "Hi," she called, still giggling. "Your sign says you have e-bikes. Can I rent one? And a rack to fit it on Harry's cab?"

BY SEVEN O'CLOCK, NO fashionable lateness for her, Elise was at La Firenze restaurant, with her rented e-bike parked in the bike rack by Harry before he took off. A cool bath and shampoo had picked her up enough to go to Fulford Harbour with Harry and drink Red Zinger tea with Sunflower in the General Store. Interesting people, she thought with a smile. Neither of them were rocket scientists, but they sure had a very acceptable level of friendly good cheer. Now if only La Firenze could live up to the quality of Sunflower's tea and cookies...

Dale was waiting inside the front door of the restaurant, dressed more neatly than she'd seen him so far, but not so much so that she felt out of place in her cotton jumpsuit. They didn't greet each other with words. Instead, Dale smiled a little (with shyness, Elise thought) and took her hand. Apology accepted.

At that moment, a grey-haired gentleman in a crisp grey suit came in with a smartly-dressed woman on his arm. Her red dress swirled as he brought her to an abrupt halt upon seeing Dale and Elise.

"Cancel our reservation," Laging told the hostess. He turned his companion around and ushered her out the door, saying: "We'll go to the Booth Bay Resort instead. They always make a place for — " The closing door cut off his words with a slam.

"No loss," said the hostess frankly. "All he eats is steak, no matter what we're serving, and he tips like a University student. Can I seat you and your friend now, Dale?"

"Certainly." With a twinkle in his eye, Dale introduced them. "May, this is my date, Elise, up from Simon Fraser University."

That set the tone for the meal, Elise felt afterwards. They were seated at the table Laging had abandoned. Their minestrone and fettuccine were served with a flourish that made Elise remember Sunflower laying out cups, kettle, teapot, honey bowl and spoons almost religiously. The hostess and waiter had the same joy in serving food that Elise had seen in a flower child older than her own grandmother. Was that common here? she asked Dale.

"It's common in good people," he replied, and they drank from glasses of wine served with the fettuccine.

Their table had six seats, and each was hand carved in a rough style and darkly stained. The back of each seat rose above the occupant's head, and showed a grimacing face. Each chair was different. Elise asked the hostess about the faces, expecting a lengthy story.

"Sorry, dear, we bought them at an auction of some Englishman's estate," answered the hostess. "They're chairs at which to seat good companions, we were told, and the faces are to scare away bad spirits, particularly unhappiness among the companions. As for where and when they were made — " she shrugged.

"I'll make you up a story, May," suggested Dale. "And you can print it on your menus. Coffee, Elise? Do you feel like having dessert?"

She shook her head. "Nothing for me, thanks." The hostess left them. "Dale, I'm crammed full of that good food. Thank you for the apology."

"Thank you for yours," he returned. "Coming here was an apology, too. I like to think that both parties should apologise — for giving and for taking offence. As we both got steamed..." he shrugged. "I'm also glad we had the chance to send Laging bouncing out of the place, driven by his own bad temper."

"I hope you didn't have plans to go dancing or to a movie," said Elise cautiously. "If there is a place to do either on the island. That walk tired me out and I want to get a lot of sleep for the morning's petroglyph expedition."

Looking a little uncomfortable, Dale began playing with the tableware. "Square dancing's not till tomorrow night, and I hate it."

Of course, realised Elise with a chill. *It's everywhere. There's no getting away from square dancers.* She looked at the gargoyle face cared on Dale's chair, and felt the silly mood slip away as quickly as it came.

"There IS a movie tonight at the community hall," Dale was saying. "But I'm afraid I have to disappoint you for tomorrow. It's my morning to work at the daycare centre."

"That's fine," she said brightly. "I rented an e-bike this afternoon. Now I can get around on my own as well. Come have a look at it — your friend at the gas station rented it to me." She had her map, and wheels of her own now. Elise was determined not to have to make another walk like that afternoon's hike back to Ganges, not if she could help it.

Paying the bill took a few moments, during which she added to the tip Dale left behind. Once outside, they scanned the little red and white e-bike, she with pride, he with some hesitancy.

"It'll get you where you're going," Dale admitted. "And there's not much traffic to collide with you. But remember any bike or moped is darned near invisible to drivers. And for cryin' out loud, try to remember that an e-bike has no acceleration compared to a car. You'll reach thirty klicks or so, tops, and it'll take a while to get up to speed."

"I think that's about my speed," said Elise. "I'm more worried about running into other people than them running into me." A little recklessly, she added, "Kiss me good night, and I'll be off."

It was an odd kiss, with her seated on the e-bike and half-twisted under his hands resting gently on her shoulders. She put a hand on the flat, hard muscles of his stomach and felt his cool brass buckle against the heel of her palm. Their lips met chastely, closed, but his lips were firm and quivered against hers. She broke the kiss before either of them needed to breathe and put on her helmet. "Good night, Dale." She rode away, still hearing his reply, as warm as his mouth had been.

She still felt reckless after riding, and free, as she arrived at her rented house. The cool air had made her sleepy, not more alert. Elise leaned the e-bike up against the house, unlocked the door and stumbled inside. She walked once through all the rooms, opening all the windows a few inches to let in fresh air. Then she went to bed and yawned her way through a chapter of *The Life of Saint Francis of Assisi*. She fell asleep without turning out the bedside lamp.

Abruptly she woke up to the same engine sound as the night before. Glancing at the clock, Elise saw that it was just after midnight. The sound of the powerful engine came closer, and roared up her driveway. Next to the house, the car screeched to a stop, and the engine began roaring wildly. The sound echoed through the small house, as the driver must have known it would.

Terror nearly froze Elise's hands, but she fumbled her way into her robe and over to the phone. Thank goodness she had put Jim Wicker's card on the table. This is no time to fumble with a phone book, she thought shakily.

"Mr Wickers? This is Elise Hammell." She swallowed, and tried to steady her voice. "There's some maniac in a big car in my driveway, revving his engine and scaring away all the sheep." *Now why did I add that?* one part of her mind said to another. "I would appreciate it if —"

"I'll be right over," came the reply. "There's a phone in my truck so I can call the RCMP if needed. Doors locked? Just sit tight then. I'm two minutes away." The phone clicked and there was dead air in her ear.

There was a sharp report from outside and the roar of the car died. Elise lay flat on the floor. "That was a backfire," she whispered to herself intently. "Gunfire is much louder and sharper and does not necessarily accompany a threatening vehicle." She sprawled under the table and listened to the starter grind and whine until the engine caught again.

This time she heard the gears shift audibly into reverse, and the car backed away, spraying gravel into the lawn. Funny how she could hear the little splats as the stones hit the grass. "I'm developing remarkable powers of observation these days," she said aloud. "*This* is a rest cure?" The anonymous car roared off towards Ganges, and as it faded, she heard the grinding rumble of what had to be Wickers' truck approaching.

Relieved, she stumbled to the door and unlocked it. Wickers' truck rocked its way into the new ruts in her driveway. She turned on the porch light as the property manager got out of the rolling truck with a baseball bat in his hand.

"You all right?" asked Wickers. She nodded dumbly. "I saw his lights go up the hill to Ganges. Whoever it was has orange tail lights," he said. "I'll just tell my wife that you're okay." He tossed the bat onto the seat and turned off the truck engine. He was saying something into a cell phone when there came the now-familiar quiet rumble of what had to be Dale's Land Rover. It turned in to her driveway on two wheels, and stopped on a dime behind the truck.

"I was coming back from Sunflower's place when I got the phone call." He took in Elise's appearance, robe and bare feet, in one glance. "What happened?"

Pulling the robe tighter around herself, she told them both. There didn't seem to be anything to bring the police out for at this time of night, and Wickers offered to make the call to the non-emergency line. She thanked him, as she began to shiver in the night air.

"I'm glad I stopped to drink a sample of Sunflower's blackberry wine," was Dale's comment. "I'd made her a new wine rack and since she's up every night till her husband comes home from the hotel, I thought —"

"Why are you chattering about Sunflower?" *Methinks he doth protest too much*, thought Elise sourly. And wrapped her arms tighter around herself.

"Because I didn't want you to think I'd drive all this way out here from my place just to drive past your place," Dale admitted.

That is one humble guy, she thought and was opening her mouth as Wickers spoke.

"I don't see why he shouldn't look in on the place now and then," he said. "My wife was on the phone to him when I left. Him being the owner and all."

There was a moment of silence.

"Owner!" screeched Elise. "When did you have time to set me up in this place?"

"I just asked Jim to show you the listing," Dale said desperately.

"I just bet! After I just put up those rubbings on the walls so the place feels like mine, now I learn it's yours?" Elise stepped inside the door, switching off the porch light. "Have fun at the daycare centre tomorrow. I hope the kids puke on you."

36

ISLAND VIEWS

The door slammed.

WHEN ELISE TOOK THE e-bike out on the road in the morning, the gravel driveway had been raked level. She didn't trouble her mind one bit wondering whether Mr Wickers or Dale had done it for her. She was off to find a petroglyph on her own today. A quick phone call to Mrs Wickers proved she really was a finder, one whose skills included where to rent a boat. Elise intended to follow her advice.

Down at the Ganges dock she rented a boat for the day. She chose one with an outboard motor. "For a real beginner," she made sure to say. Buckling on a life jacket, she decided to tie her duffle bag to the seat. It was waterproof but it wouldn't float, she figured. Then she unfolded the simple map Dale had given her yesterday — no, two days ago, now — and made her plan.

Goat Island was probably not a good choice. It was the nearest tiny island in Ganges Harbour, and she figured it would be popular all summer. The next island out was smaller, and seemed more likely. The name was Deadman Island. *Yeugh*, she thought. *The name alone is probably enough to keep people away*. Briefly she wondered if she had any idea yet of the size and distance of these islands, but as she looked out from the dock she could clearly see both Goat Island and Deadman. She could probably even swim back in a pinch.

It was a pleasant trip, humming low over the water alone. There were a few sailboats coming into the harbour but no others leaving the dock, Elise noticed. A stony beach on the near side of Deadman Island seemed a natural place to land, so she did, pulling the boat partway up onto the beach. She had faced the sunniest part of the sky on the way over and hadn't realised what a grey day it was this morning. No matter, she was wearing a windbreaker that could shed a little rain if necessary. She untied the duffle bag and set out to find rocks like those Dale had shown her.

For an hour she looked without success. Even the flat shale of a jutting point of land had no carvings, and she had crawled over and checked it from different angles as the tide went out. Still, Elise was sure that this particular little islet had been a good choice. It was small enough to walk all the way around and inspect thoroughly without the walk taking too long. Half-way round the circuit again she stopped to let a green sea anemone suck on her fingertip. Then she made to stand up, and saw it.

A petroglyph! She'd found it on her own. Elise didn't hope for more than a minute that it was a new one no one else knew about. Probably it was as well known as the one in Drummond Park, she figured, and got out a sheet of coarse paper and the black pad.

The design came up in a few strokes. It was a face, with nose, eyes, and brows, and one splayed hand beside it. *Not bad at all*, she decided, and stored it in the mailing tube.

She stood up and stretched. Was there time to look for another? Maybe it would be better to check on her boat and have a bite to eat first. Breakfast hadn't appealed to her that morning, with all the grey light coming in her west and south windows, so she really should eat now.

When she looked across the boat's small open frame, she saw white capped waves in the harbour, and a curtain of rain advancing down the hills of Saltspring to the water's edge. It looked like no matter what, she'd get rained on before she got halfway across the harbour.

Food seemed like a priority for the moment. She'd eat first, Elise decided, and see how the weather was doing then, if it was any better or worse.

It was worse. She munched on raisins and sausage from the deli and finished a can of Coke before the rain hit. Advancing with the sheets of rain was a powered boat much larger than the one she had rented.

Someone else out in the rain? Maybe they'll give me a lift back. The thought suddenly occurred to her that maybe she'd *need* a lift back to the dock.

"Oh man," she groaned. "I thought I'd planned this out." The rain hit her then, a thousand tiny cold drops, and she shivered.

The other boat came to a stop about a hundred feet offshore, so she pushed her own boat off the beach and climbed in, wet feet and all. It took only a few moments before she brought her boat close to the bigger one. When a rope was thrown to her, she tied the end to a metal ring set in the bow of her boat. Then her Good Samaritan tugged on the rope and pulled her boat tight against the larger boat.

It was Dale, of course.

"Why you would risk your neck when a storm is coming on is beyond me," he snapped. "All right, so hand me the duffle bag first. Now get in this boat. Move it!"

Startled, she moved quickly and lightly over the gunwales and into the larger boat, mostly lifted by the hand Dale held in a firm grip. His blunt, rounded nails were white under the pressure he exerted. She guessed he was leaving a bruise, but it was better than falling overboard.

"Did you think to get a chart? Or a radio?" he asked, starting his boat's engine up again and heading for shore. Wordlessly, Elise held up the road map and her cell phone that was in her duffle. Dale snorted. "That's good for music, but no good for sending messages out in the harbour where there's no WiFi." He didn't speak again till they were docked at a small marina, not the government docks nor the place where she had rented her boat.

Once both boats were tied up, Dale grabbed her arm again. They ran together along the dock to shore where the Land Rover was parked. They climbed in. She was too wet and apathetic to listen to what Dale was saying on his cell phone, except for the last part.

"I've brought her in. Your boat is tied up behind mine at the sailing club. If you're stupid and inconsiderate enough to rent a boat to a beginner when it's about to rain, you can go and get it yourself. I'm done."

With that he turned his cell phone off and drove the Land Rover away from the sailing club.

"I was buying some pastry to take to a friend this afternoon," Dale said without looking at her. "Mrs Blaus told me about your expedition. You can either come to my place to dry off and warm up, or come with me to my friend's place. Any preference?"

"The friend's place, certainly. There hasn't been a dull one in the lot yet." Elise felt a dripping on her head. "It's raining in here! It's raining harder than it is outside!"

"This is a desert vehicle. It's made to keep out dust and sand. Water is another thing entirely."

"This is crazy! I'm more in danger of drowning now than before." She looked over to see his glower evaporate.

"You are if you keep bad mouthing my car," he grinned finally. Then, more hesitantly, "Sorry you had no luck."

"What? No, I found one! You probably know all about it," she chattered, beginning to realise how cold she had become. "But I looked for it like you showed me, and there it was."

"Speaking of there it is," interrupted Dale. "This is my place we're passing now. The neighbour ahead is the friend we're visiting. Try not to get his heart rate kicked up too high, will you? He likes the 'pretty young things,' as he'd call you." Dale saw her glare and added quickly, "I wouldn't call you that, Ms Hammell."

Elise turned her attention to the property passing by. It looked to be a large field surrounded by thick forest on three sides, with four sturdy sheds built close to the road and a mobile home set behind them. "It looks nice, what I can see of it," she said. "How far does it go back?"

"Through the trees halfway to the ocean." Dale turned in to the next driveway and parked near that house. He grabbed a grocery bag from the back seat. "Okay, I've got strudels here to share. Get ready to run through the rain... Go!" They shot out and up to the door.

After a quick knock, Dale opened the door and rushed Elise in out of the rain. "Hello, Mark, I'm here!" he called. "Hope you have pants on, cuz I've brought a lady to visit."

Before Elise was really aware of it, she'd been handed a large, soft towel by a small man wearing a tweed suit. Gratefully, she dried her head, pulled off her squall jacket, and dried her arms and hands. She'd wriggled into a sweater from her bag before noticing the attentive way Mark was looking at her.

The little man sighed. "Nice to meet you," he said to Elise. To Dale he added, "It's so lovely to see them move, don't you think? I have a carving of a woman pulling a sweater off over her head, but I think a woman putting clothes on is just as interesting."

"Elise drinks tea," Dale said, and that was their introduction.

Half an hour's chatter over tea and apple strudels later, she had heard all about some carvings Mark had done into the burls of old trees on his property. "That was years ago," he said, picking a flake of pastry from his tweeds. "But they're still visible, if you squint a little. What's much more interesting are the stone carvings a local First Nations artist did for my father years before that. There are a dozen of them scattered about the place."

"Does anything in your hobby say the petroglyphs have to be from pre-colonial times? Not all of the carvings in the parks are that old." Dale waited for Elise's answer.

She thought about it and shrugged. "It's not important to me how old the carving is, I don't think, as long as it's First Nations work. That's an idea — I'll ask the nearest band council where the petroglyphs are around here. They must have a good idea how many of them there are."

Mark and Dale were shaking their heads. "It doesn't work that way, Elise," Dale told her. He bit into another strudel and managed to catch a gob of apple filling as it fell from his lip.

"How many churches are there in the town you grew up in?" asked Mark, handing Dale a paper napkin. "Or art galleries? People don't always talk about the cultural things a visitor wants to ask after. Many people living on a reserve don't know exactly where and how many petroglyphs there are. The ones who do know might not like being questioned by a stranger."

"I guess it's something I never had to understand before. Don't want to be rude." She thought about it for a while. "I guess, then, I'd better be happy with what I can find on the island with Dale's help. I wonder if anyone's disappointed by finding recently carved petroglyphs."

"Well, the federal government is," said Mark, taking another strudel from Dale's package. "Some officials have been treating the carvings like untouchably sacred objects, or some manner of miniature Stonehenge, to be seen and contemplated by people of European ancestry, but never understood. Now it turns out some of these stones are more on the order of graffiti. That's inconvenient for some officials who insist on reliable categories for everything. Is it an art form or a religious artifact? What if it's carved onto a stone under the Government dock?" He reached for the teapot. "Of course, the only people really upset are the collectors."

He had poured each of them tea before either of the others spoke.

"Collectors?" squeaked Elise, a second before Dale.

"I'm afraid so. Some unscrupulous dealers are selling petroglyphs to New York art fanciers as prehistoric art."

"Elise knows someone who has one in his living room," Dale informed him.

"I never thought of him as a collector, or a dealer in them," she stammered. "He had just the one stone there, and talked about it. Said it was a good object lesson for understanding the human within, but he was bored and wanted a new one." She didn't say anything more for a while, but neither of the men questioned her. They all had mouths full of strudel.

They left Mark when the rain stopped and headed back to the docks for Elise's e-bike. Without argument from her, Dale lifted it into the back of the Land Rover and drove her home.

"Didn't you buy marshmallows the other day?" he asked as they neared her house. "If I light the stove, can we toast some?"

"Why don't you just ask to stay for dinner? If you eat omelettes, you'll like my cooking. I can't think of marshmallows yet after all that strudel, but lighting the stove does sound good to me."

It was getting dark by the time they entered the little house. Elise turned on the lights and stared in bewilderment at the kitchen walls. There were no coarse paper rubbings there anymore, the thumbtacks fallen to the floor.

"Dale... who else has a key to this place?" she asked with a sinking feeling.

He spoke from the living room, seeming at first totally unaware of what she had said. "You didn't tell me you'd already lit the stove. There are ashes in here, and it's always swept out between tenants." He came into the kitchen and looked through a drawer for the matches, finally coming up with a box. "Um, nobody has a key except for Wickers and me. He's really good about making sure that tenants return their copies. That's not my department, that's Wickers' job. Why, what's up?"

"Somebody came in and burned my petroglyph rubbings," Elise said dully. She felt such loss for what were essentially just cheap pieces of paper from an art supply store. But they were hers, dammit!

Dale's jaw dropped. "Somebody broke into my place —" he corrected himself, "*your* place to burn some handmade posters? It doesn't make sense." Quickly, he checked all the windows and returned to the kitchen, where she sat staring at the one rubbing she had left. It was the one she made that morning at Deadman Island and had in her duffle bag.

"None of the windows have been forced," he reported. "I think you're right. It must have been someone with a key."

"Are any of the former tenants still on the island?" This time her questions lacked her normal bright inquiring nature. She turned the black-coloured pad from her art kit over and over in her hands.

"Not many. There's Sunflower's old man, he stayed here for a while when they had a fight, and um... some real estate agent, what's her name." He gestured pointlessly. "She's in her forties, likes to dress in red."

A warning bell went off in Elise's mind. "Does she date J. Vaughn Laging?"

With a sick snap Dale's eyes locked on hers. "Uh-huh. She was his dining companion last night when Laging ran out of La Firenze. You don't think —"

"I don't know what to think," she said wearily. "But it's being strongly suggested that I rethink spending all this time with you and with petroglyphs." She raised the black pad as if to drop it on the rubbing. "Maybe I ought to see Wickers in the morning about getting a refund and then head back to Vancouver. The Stanley Park Zoo might have a job opening by now."

"No." He took the pad from her hand before it could blot the rubbing, and put it away in her bag. "Tomorrow, maybe you ought to go to the Sunset Gallery and look through the art prints and oil paintings and see if you can find any of these rubbings done on fabric. They're supposed to be much more effective for interior decorating. And then maybe you'd like me to take you to the Fulford Inn for a cold, dry apple cider with lime." His hand dropped gently on her hair. "Does that sound any better?"

Elise put her head in her hands. *Think, think!* Her brain felt like mush. How much of what Dale told her could she trust, after all? He had enough friends that he could have sent someone to get in here while she was off drinking tea on Mark's tweed-upholstered couch.

"I don't know. It sounds fine. Let me be for a minute."

She heard him step back and start working on something or other behind her. When at last she looked up, it was to the smell of frying eggs and cheese. He was cooking for her?

"Omelette sound okay?" He was slicing a tomato. "Let's try a Mexican version, shall wee? With a little hot sauce and lots more cheese if you have any mozzarella."

Before she knew it she was setting the table. They sat together. They ate together. They didn't talk much. They toasted marshmallows at the Franklin stove in the living room and watched the flames because there was no television set.

And then Dale turned towards her and offered to sleep in his Land Rover in case the driver who had come by to rev his engine might make another visit. Elise gave him a quilt, sent him out, and locked the door. Her sleep was very deep and without dreams of any interest at all. There was no interruption from any night travellers.

WHEN HE KNOCKED ON the door, bleary-eyed and rumpled from sleeping in his clothes, she had coffee made and waiting for him. "Rise and shine," she sang. "I just figured a way to sting Laging for a few bucks, even if he isn't the one who has been hassling me."

"Oh yeah? Lay it on me." Dale took the coffee from her and drank half of it in one gulp.

"I'm going to show my student card at the gallery's sales counter, and insist on a student discount, even though I've graduated and it isn't valid any longer."

"Nice to see you've got your sense of humour back," he said sourly. "Anybody ever tell you that you make lousy coffee?"

"You know a better place this time of day?"

He knew a better place, of course. They were in the Land Rover and half-way there before she finished lacing her hiking boots.

The bakery he led her to was open, and full of the warm smell of fresh croissants. They ate standing up, trying to catch the crumbs. Dale swore by their coffee. "Whenever I go out to work in the morning, it's the only thing that gets me there," he insisted, hamming it up for the clerk.

Elise poured herself a final cup of tea into her travel mug, from the Brown Betty pot on the counter. They went back to the Land Rover. "And now, to beard the lion in his den."

"Speaking of bearding," said Dale as he drove. "I'm going to drop you off there and go home to shave. Will an hour be long enough to poke through the gallery?"

"You're going to leave me alone with that island eccentric? He might be the madman who tried to scare me the other night." She drank her tea. "Will the place even be open this early?"

The vehicle bumped along a road beside a large lake. "Sure it will! This is Sunday. Laging opens the place early on weekends for the tourists." Dale pulled over in front of what was obviously the Sunset Gallery: parking lot, gardens, large house with a big square addition tacked on in front, and dense trees behind. "Besides, if he's forced to talk to me, he might really live up to the title of 'island eccentric.' Can you just picture my skin as a tiger rug? 'Shot him in Injah, y'know.' I'll see you later."

Elise wandered around the gardens for ten minutes until the doors were officially unlocked by a girl young enough to be in high school. Then she walked back, past the rock garden Dale had made. Funny, he had never mentioned using rocks with petroglyphs for the garden. Oh well, it wasn't like him to tell everything anyways.

The gallery was cool and classy, with the kind of exhibition she had come to despise from seeing too many on campus. Still lifes in oil on canvas. Pencil and charcoal sketches of barns falling down. Tasteful female nudes. Elise asked to be shown the petroglyph rubbings, and felt better. She took her time selecting a cloth wall hanging with the same design as the first rubbing she had made, now ashes.

It'll look good above the Franklin stove, she told herself, as she paid the bill (less a 15% student discount). *If I stay,* another voice said in her head.

She dismissed both voices and tried to keep on an even keel. Maybe she'd get her e-bike and go for pizza later. Maybe Sunflower knew where there were more petroglyphs. Maybe.

There were a lot of maybes coming up, and she didn't want to miss any of them. Elise took up her bag with no smile of thanks to the clerk, and went out to look for Dale.

He was waiting in the parking lot, whistling at a jay beside the road.

"Dale," she said as she put her bag in the Land Rover. "Why didn't you mention using petroglyphs in the rock garden? There's a real nice one there, just like the one I found yesterday."

"I didn't use any stones with carvings," he answered with a frown. "I know that, because I became intimately acquainted with each and every one of those rocks. Oh, my aching back."

"Well, there's one there now. On the gravel beside the parking lot."

"Show me." Dale took her by the arm and this time she didn't shrug away. "If Laging has been humping rocks up into his own garden, this I gotta see."

Elise snorted. "Picture an old man like that carrying rocks around."

"People can go grey at thirty, Elise." He was checking out the rock garden, with careful glances towards the house and the Lincoln Continental parked a few feet from the garden. "Laging is forty-nine. That's hardly ancient. Didn't you look at him in the restaurant?"

"I only had eyes for you," she sang, but stopped when he straightened abruptly.

"There's no carving here, on any of the loose or fixed stones."

"But it was right here," Elise turned around, puzzled. "Why would the back end of an expensive car like this sag down so far? Does he really mistreat his car so much?" She walked past the orange tail lights and reached out to put a hand on the fender.

"Don't touch it! There's a contact alarm on the car." Dale was looking at the car's low back end. "How big was that rock? Can you remember?"

"I could have rolled it, or gotten my arms around it, but lifting it would be out of the question." Her brain stopped working, and her mouth kept flapping. "You don't think —"

He grinned. "I do think. In fact, I think I know why Laging was trying to talk a friend of *mine* out of an interest in petroglyphs. He's been bringing them here and dumping them beside the rock garden, like just another stone. No wonder he doesn't want me around anymore. I might count the stones."

"This is really too much." She started back to the car. "Let me know when you come back to the real world. What would he do with a bunch of petroglyphs in his garden? Write poems about them like your friend Mark?"

Dale hissed at her across the seat as they got into the Land Rover. "Sell them to collectors! Those rich do-nothings with big yachts and private penthouse suites crammed with native art, and modern art, and anything creative enough that they don't understand it."

That rang true, as Elise remembered the party in her professor's apartment and the petroglyph he had negligently draped with a Guatemalan weaving. She dropped her gaze to the strangely shaped brass buckle of Dale's belt and found she couldn't disagree. "So what do we do now?"

"We go up the road a ways and wait," he told her, with a wicked smile. "Laging won't leave that rock in his trunk long, it'll ruin the shocks. He'll either head past us to Fernwood dock, or... Will you look at that? We don't even have to wait. He must have been in a real hurry."

The magenta Lincoln turned to the south and sped off in a cloud of blue exhaust. Dale started the Land Rover and followed, trying to work his cell phone and the gear shift with the same hand. Elise listened with half an ear, heart pounding with growing excitement.

A car chase! She was actually in a car chase. High speeds, powerful engines, the works. She combed her hair and arranged her scarf to flutter with the breeze from the window. *Might as well look the part*, she decided.

"Yeah, Chris, I know there are only two of you working today. Where are you, at Long Harbour or Fulford Harbour?" Dale was saying into his phone. "But if you send one of you over to Musgrave Landing NOW, and like I mean *right now*, you just might be in time to see a large parcel change hands." There was a garble of words from the phone that Elise didn't catch, but Dale seemed to understand it. "No, it isn't drugs this time. Get a move on, Chris. Getting a Customs vehicle over that mountain isn't going to be quick. I want you to have as much lead time as possible. Meet you there." He hung up the call and grinned at her. "Feel like a gun moll in a black and white movie yet? Or maybe a lady detective?"

"Why did I wear my hiking boots to a bust?" she wailed. "Can we stop at my place so I can change?"

"Quit laughing. Busts are come-as-you-are." He slowed the vehicle while passing through Ganges village, then picked up speed again as they passed a daycare centre. "There's where I was working yesterday," he pointed out.

She dropped the comedy. "How can you be so calm?"

For answer, he held out a hand for a moment so that she could see his tremor. "That man has kept me from more electrical work with all this construction going on... He's made no secret of his dislike for me, and if I can make him squirm under a few questions from a Canada Customs official, I want to be there to see him squirm!"

They took a corner on three wheels, and Elise clutched the seat. "I'm glad I left my e-bike behind, but am I going to need the helmet?"

"Relax. I haven't rolled this baby yet, and I don't intend to."

Roaring down a long slope, they saw the Lincoln ahead, scaring the sheep again with the sound of its engine. "Poor skinny sheep," she commented as they went past the pasture. "Whoever owns them is going to get pretty lean mutton."

"Another grievance against the evil J. Vaughn Laging," snarled Dale. "Scourge of sheep farmers and itinerant... um, what am I?" he appealed to her.

"The black sheep of a well-to-do family," she retorted.

"That's three!" He sketched another mark on his imaginary blackboard, then whipped his hand back to the wheel for another turn.

"Will you lay off on that counting! Do you think he knows we're following him?"

Dale glared at her as they rocked and bumped past Drummond Park. "Elise! We have only been tailing him from Saint Mary Lake all the way down here in one of the more distinctive vehicles on Saltspring Island. I would have borrowed Sunflower's Volkswagen bug, but I think lavender clashes with magenta." They rounded a sharp corner and began climbing. "And I do want this car chase to be classy and memorable."

"There have been others? What was that you said to Chris about drugs?" Elise put her duffle bag under the seat where it wouldn't keep rolling around.

"I don't worry about people trading a little grass around here. That's mostly legal," said Dale, shifting the engine's purr into a four-wheel drive rumble. "But when Keefer told me about some people sending a bale over to some kids for a junior-high party in Victoria, we put a word in Chris's ear, yes."

She felt admiration for him stir again. "So speaks the loyal daycare worker."

"It's a job. A human skill. I try to be able to do as many things as a person can, even change diapers." He took the Land Rover around a switchback corner with a crossroad coming into the bend. "You ought to try it, Ms Hammell. It's very humanizing."

Movement in the rear view mirror caught Elise's attention. "He's coming up behind us!"

Hard on their bumper, the Lincoln forced them into accelerating as the road suddenly took a turn down. They were now hurtling down the mountain they had just climbed. She felt her stomach lurch. "I am NOT going to be sick," she announced, and clung tighter to the seat.

"For pity's sake, woman, keep quiet!" Dale roared again as he had done before, but this time the theatrical quality was completely gone from it. She saw his hand, and focussed on his oval fingernails gripping the gear shift, forcing it down a gear. "He's trying to run us off the road!"

The two cars jockeyed back and forth, tires squealing on several turns as the road dropped more than three hundred feet in less than a mile. Elise kept her opinions about her stomach to herself. She heard Dale muttering under his breath.

"One bag of white plaster, ten gallons warm water, and a box of cream of tartar," he said through his teeth. "Stir thoroughly with a plastering hoe and let the heat dissipate. The trowel should be —"

He's mixing plaster, she realised. I never knew he was a plasterer, too. One of my uncles is a plasterer, I should find out how steady the work is... She took a firm hold of herself, wiped her hands and got a better grip on the seat. *Quit seeing him in a romantic light,* she told herself. *It's just another of those things he's done for a year or two and left behind. He probably wouldn't even finish building a house.* But another voice in her head said clearly, over all the grinding of gears and squealing tires: *You take a hard-working man wherever you find him. Even in a different job every year. He'll keep you interested.*

At that moment the Land Rover skidded sideways off the narrow road, into a steep gully, and rolled over twice.

THEY LANDED, FINALLY, upright on the wheels and rocked several times. At some point during the wild tumble the motor had stalled. Too terrified to move, Elise heard the engine's quiet, rhythmic ticking. She drew a shuddering breath and screamed, full-throated, loud and long. It was full of terror, and shock, and a wild instant rage against everything that had put her here.

"I'm sorry, baby, I never meant to put you through this," Dale was whispering. "You weren't made for this, baby, I'm sorry, I should never have taken you up here."

His quiet voice calmed her. She was able to turn and look at him, feeling gratitude and a wild fire of emotion running through her body.

He was talking to his car, one strong hand on the dashboard and the other on the gear shift.

She screamed again, and it was at least as satisfying as the first time. He flinched, and whispered, "Oh God, I've killed her."

"*You're* not so lucky," Elise said, her throat raw and husky. "Now what are we going to do?"

"You're not hurt?"

"Not for lack of opportunity, but —"

He hit the release catch on her safety belt and pulled her into his arms. She felt the hard hands that had kept his desert vehicle on the road for so long take hold on her body and hold it beyond resistance. When his mouth lifted at last from hers, there were the bruises the fall had not been able to make. Elise moved only to press her swollen lips against his skin and feel the corded muscles in his neck against her mouth. He held her to him, not rocking her like a child, and she felt the rhythm of his pulse wash over her. Its wake left her trembling, disturbed.

His hands began to move. "There's a gear shift in your back," Dale said softly. He made to lower his head again, but she twisted free.

"Where are we, Dale? Halfway down the mountain?"

He let her go. "Almost halfway down Mount Tuam. I told you when we met I'd take you down it at a hundred klicks and roll us off a couple of rocks. Well, the old speedometer's shattered at sixty-five miles an hour. Close enough."

She looked out the front window at the thick bushes growing in the gully. "How are we going to get out of here?"

He unbuckled his safety belt and stepped out. "That part's no trouble. We climb up the gully, me with the end of this steel cable in my hand. If there are no obstacles on the way up, and a secure tree at the top to anchor the cable, I can even get the Land Rover out of here with the winch."

Climbing up a gully on a West Coast island was not as easy as it sounded. The salal here grew taller than Elise, just as promised. She used the tough, slender branches for handholds and footholds. Once again it was a good thing she was wearing hiking boots, she realised. After a few minutes of wrestling her way up the steep slope, she looked down to see that the ground was several feet below her boots.

"How strong is this salal?" she panted.

"Strong enough, but flexible. Work your way along so you can get at least one foot on the ground," Dale advised, climbing like a monkey. The cable didn't seem to be slowing him down at all. He passed her and continued up towards the road.

So much for chivalry. But, she reminded herself, she hadn't asked for help. Pressing on, she climbed past some plant that bristled with spines and scratched her all down one leg, hundreds of prickles right through her jeans. *A devil's club*, she guessed.

That wasn't enough of a challenge. Just as she finally got clear of the spiny menace, Elise reached for a new handhold and shrieked. Something was clinging to the branch in front of her.

"DALE!" It was green and black and coated with a sort of slime, from what she could stand to see of it. "There's something here that's — ugh, it's moving! Dale!"

She heard the crash of his approach before his words. "I'm coming, I'm coming..." He slid to a stop beside her, ready for bear. "What, where, what is it?" Elise pointed. She had no words left. Whatever the slimy thing was grew wiggly antenna on one end.

He stared, then looked back at her, disgusted. "That," he said, "is a slug. A plain old banana slug. No uglier than most. Bigger than some. *This* you can't handle?"

"Slugs are little things like my thumbnail. I've seen them back home in Scarborough. This is a slug?" She moved around it carefully and continued up the gully. "That's the biggest slug I've ever heard of. And the ugliest thing I've ever seen. How big are the cockroaches around here?"

"We don't have many of them," Dale called back cheerfully. He climbed faster and was almost at the road again. "Now, down in Florida, roaches are almost as big as your hand. They call them palmetto bugs."

If I didn't throw up during that wild ride, Elise told herself, *nothing will nauseate me again. Not even ugly slugs*. Eventually she struggled up to the road and pulled herself up to lie, gasping, on the shoulder. She saw the cable fastened to a tree across the road but no Dale. He had gone back down the gully and she had not even heard him go by.

She heard the winch, though, when Dale started the Land Rover. In a slow crawl, the battered machine pulled itself up and out from where it had rolled. The climb took ages and by the time he was unfastening the cable, Elise had finger-combed her hair, shaken the leaves and dirt off her clothes as much as she could, and touched her bruised lips, almost with awe. She got quietly into the passenger seat and buckled in, careful not to brush against Dale.

They proceeded down the mountain road, no longer at a break-neck pace. She supposed he was trying to nurse the engine along, probably tallying up what repairs might be needed and how much they would cost. She looked over and saw him brush the back of his hand thoughtfully against his mouth.

"How did you know that Laging was headed for Musgrave Landing?" she asked quickly.

Dale's eyes focused more sharply and he sat up straighter. "Oh. That wasn't hard. Musgrave Landing has a good harbour for bringing a big yacht right up to the dock when the tide is high. It's the only dock like that on the southern half of the island that doesn't also have a customs official or ferry terminal or something similarly troublesome for a smuggler."

"No wonder the Lincoln is always in the shop for maintenance and repairs. Your friend at the service station told me she checks the oil, brakes, shocks, and tires every time Laging comes in for gas." She shook her head. "I believe it, if he's always taking this road."

"I know what you're not saying to me," Dale kept his eyes on the road. "We'll talk about it later. For now, I guess it's too much to hope for, to see Laging getting busted for smuggling."

They rode in silence through the green woods until Dale parked the Land Rover. Ahead, at the end of the road, Elise could see the glint of water. "Come on," he said. "Let's not advertise our presence. The motor's not running as quietly as it used to." They didn't walk hand in hand, although she did let him take her arm to help her down a steeply slanted walkway to the dock.

It was easy to guess which boat Laging had been planning to meet. It was a three-masted sailing vessel with dark-stained wood and polished brass everywhere Elise looked. The sails were furled and the boat securely moored to the far part of the dock, where several figures were standing. One wore sailing clothes, as Elise thought of them, and turned away from the other two to jump aboard his vessel. As Elise and Dale approached, she could see the other two people more clearly.

One was a young man with a brush cut, a light blue uniform, and a scowl. Obviously he was the Customs official, Elise deduced. Elementary, my dear Wallis. The other had steel-grey hair and was gesturing angrily. That would be J. Vaughn Laging, if bad temper was any guide.

Behind Laging on the dock stood a small dolly with a sturdy crate. Bingo.

She looked at Dale as he smiled, showing sharp teeth. "So I got to see it after all," he said, with a thirst she'd heard only the shadow of until now.

At that moment, Laging threw up his hands in frustration, spun, and picked up the crate. He lifted it easily but carefully, legs taking the load and shoulders almost splitting his linen sports jacket. He turned round with it. Obviously he intended simply to walk on board the sailing vessel and be done with the argument, when he happened to see Dale. Their glances locked.

It was then that Laging started to crumple at the knees. His mouth quivered but his eyes stayed hard as the crate slipped slowly from his arms. Laging clutched at his left arm as the crate broke open at his feet. It was clearly visible to Elise from where she stood that his eyes were now focused on some inward place, some private introspection.

He toppled forward across the broken crate. As the Customs official caught him, the stone rolled forth from the shattered wood and lurched in a crazy circle at his feet.

Dale sighed. "Scratch one opponent." He broke into a run, with Elise racing to keep up with him.

BETWEEN DALE AND CHRIS they got the big man up the steep walkway and into the customs vehicle. Elise loosened his collar as Dale made a call on his cell phone for an ambulance to come out from the small hospital in Ganges. Chris shook his head when told the ambulance was on its way.

"Tell them I'll beat them coming over the mountain and meet them coming this way, or I'll give up my job and go fishing for the rest of my days. There's no way this guy's getting out of a sticky situation. I'm going to enjoy keeping him alive," he said, with an enthusiasm that went beyond getting the job done. Chris set out on the return trip with his almost unconscious passenger.

When the dust from his wheels settled, Elise looked up at Dale. "Isn't he enjoying this arrest a little too much? We *are* talking about a heart attack here. For a moment I thought you had the evil eye."

"Yeah," said Dale, looking up the road. "But then, you couldn't hear what Chris was muttering into Laging' ear while we were frog-marching him along. Apparently Chris's little sister works at the Sunset Gallery. I guess Laging got a bit inappropriate, not expecting her to be the talkative type."

"Yuck. And I thought nothing could nauseate me after that ride." Elise resolved to be nicer to that young clerk when their paths crossed again.

He took her arm gently and walked with her back down the slanting walkway onto the dock where the petroglyph rock lay. The boat owner had given all his identification papers to Chris and was holed up inside his boat, polishing grommets for all they knew. They were alone with the stone she had seen on Deadman Island.

Dale guided her gently to sit on the dock where she could see the carving clearly. He sat near her, but not too close. "Now talk," he said. "Tell me what you haven't been telling me. More about why you came here. More about what these stones mean to you. More about why you don't want me to touch you."

When she said nothing for a while, he went on. "It isn't about your body and your personal space. That's your right, to do with them as you like — you know it, I know it. It's that you're gradually leaning towards me, then leaping away. I want to understand it. Can you please talk to me?"

Helplessly, she spread her hands.

"Where did you get your belt buckle?" she asked.

"I made it." He turned a little and hung his legs over the end of the dock. "When I was in shop class we got the chance to cast brass, so I made this belt buckle for myself. Used the lost wax method. I was fifteen that year."

"And where did you get that design?" She couldn't look at him. Instead, she looked across the water to the great mountains on Vancouver Island. The sun was starting to lower in that direction.

"That summer, I came here on my own. Mrs Blaus let me have room and board with her. I ran wild all over the island. It began to feel like home that year. Later when my parents realised I'd never care to manage the family business, they gave me their few pieces of property here. So I'd always be provided for, was how my mother put it." He laced his big, neat hands together and looked at them. "One day that summer I was fifteen, I found a petroglyph. It was the first one I ever saw on my own. It wasn't trapped like that one in Drummond Park between the trees with a sign next to it. I don't know if anyone else has ever seen it. I haven't been able to find it again. I don't care. It's mine and I keep it here." He patted the brass buckle. "That's like you, to get me talking with your questions instead of answering mine. Your turn, eh?"

"I spent four years getting credit for what I had already read, and learned, and knew," Elise said slowly. "I was supposed to be making myself new memories and finding a solid footing for my own life and interests. Instead I spent four years doing precisely what I did that five weeks with the comic books: holing up without eating. Oh, a little bright chatter, some plot and characters, but really nothing to change me or keep my interest after the brightness faded."

She turned to hang her own feet over the edge of the dock. "When I saw that petroglyph in my professor's house I just drank it in. It hit me like nothing had in four years of searching for my own new ground. I let the graduation party wander in and out of the rooms around me and just sat where I could see and touch it. It was old, I could see that. Not new like the ones on Mark's land. One of the old and meaningful ones. Eventually the prof came to sit by me and tell me about the people who had carved it. 'Would I like to see more carvings like this?' he asked."

She cleared her throat. "I said 'yes, oh yes, where are they?' and he laughed. He told me some of them were here, but they were also all up and down the Coast. And, if I liked, I could hunt them down in odd places and find ones never registered before."

"That was the word that didn't fit into all that hazy golden memory. Registered. He suggested that I keep careful notes when I told him I was going on a petroglyph expedition. He even gave me a little notebook to keep with my rubbing gear, and told me to get a good chart of the coastline of each island I explored. We'll have a little conference when you get back, he said, and squeezed me around the shoulders. With affection, I thought then. Now, I don't know." Elise dug into her duffle bag and brought out a little spiral bound notebook. Dale took it from her hand. "I think he wanted me to do — what Laging has been doing. Whenever I thought about it I got sick and hated myself and anything that reminded me of it."

Dale was turning the pages of the little notebook. "This book is blank," he said. "You've written nothing in it, not even from your trip to Deadman Island with that road map for a guide."

"It's not all blank. I drew a sketch of what the carving looked like on the first petroglyph I ever saw."

The first page bore a pencilled design, the twin to that on Dale's belt buckle.

"You see..." She could feel the blush rising and descending from her heart until she felt on fire everywhere. "When I saw that belt buckle you linked in my mind with all that that stone had meant. And I resented it. I wanted to know you for who you were, not follow you around like some hero, thinking of what that carving did for me, starved like I was. But when I saw that pattern my attention fixed on you, and my heart hammered." Painfully, she swallowed, and went on. "And I felt you were part of me, like all the books I'd ever read and all the music I'd ever heard. I've been fighting that feeling. Sometimes you made it easy." She smiled, remembering twenty-seven choruses of a Monty Python song which she no longer named even in her thoughts.

"Don't say it," he groaned. "I can see headlines now: Man blows his chance by singing comedy sketch. Photos on page three."

"But Dale," she said painfully, "you were also interesting. I have found so very little that's new to interest me in what feels like a long time." She wiped her eyes. When Dale put an arm around her she leaned against him. It was good to feel his side against hers, and the warm beat of his pulse on her skin where she had grown cool. She rubbed her bare arms.

"Getting cold?" His tone was light. "The wind is picking up a bit. We'll head back soon. But first..." Gently he guided her head around until she faced him. But instead of a kiss like that in the Land Rover, he laid his cheek against hers and they were close. Close enough that she could smell his clean sweat from their climb out of the gully. She could even smell a trace of soap from his shave that morning. His hair felt soft on her closed eyelids.

I could get to know him from holding him like this, Elise realised. *I could know his heart, and feelings, and what puts the salt sweat on his body, and whether his heart jumps when he thinks of me.*

The pulse in his throat began to beat roughly against her cheekbone, and he straightened. "So, does this mean we're an item in Mrs Blaus' gossip roster?" he asked lightly.

"Dale, it's been four days. I — I can't really know you yet, we've been playing at so much instead of just being together." Elise let him help her to her feet. "I declared my infatuation with you, not love."

"I know that, Elise," he said in that same light tone. "But let's give Mrs Blaus something to talk about anyways, shall we? You've got three weeks' rent paid on that house and electric bike. I hope you'll spend at least part of it letting me infatuate you more thoroughly."

He unbuckled his belt and fastened it over her clothes, around her waist at a carefree angle. "This will set you free of being pulled in two directions," he said. "I'll sink or swim on my own, without any help or harm from it."

Her eyes started stinging again. She smiled anyways. When he brought the little dolly around, she helped roll the stone onto it. She led the way up the ramp while he pushed the dolly up to the shore.

"Now I'll take you to Fulford Inn for that pint of dry apple cider with lime," he told her. "We've earned it. Chris can pick up the rock from my place when he gets around to it, if he's going to run off like that and leave it rolling around on a dock. First the cider. Then my place for dinner and to show you around my workshops. Then tomorrow after I work, we can poke around Mark's place and find the carvings in the trees and rocks." He looked at her sideways then, with a little tug on her hand. "Sound okay?"

"Well..." she drawled. "I *am* going to Sunflower's tomorrow for more Red Zinger tea."

"All right! Tomorrow we discuss tomorrow. For now, the inn." Together they lifted the stone into the back of the Land Rover.

When the engine wouldn't turn over, they used his cell phone to call Harry and SS Cabs, then sat on the hood of the Land Rover and laughed till the stars began to appear in the deepening sky.

Don't miss out!

Visit the website below and you can sign up to receive emails whenever Paula Johanson publishes a new book. There's no charge and no obligation.

https://books2read.com/r/B-A-ZKUK-CKKGB

BOOKS 2 READ

Connecting independent readers to independent writers.

Did you love *Island Views*? Then you should read *Plum Tree*[1] by Paula Johanson!

Driving with her Dad to visit Aunt May is his idea of how to help Tina out of a depression that's lasted months. But the highway is boring, the weather is hot, and she's seen enough rocks and sticks for a lifetime. Tina is so preoccupied with her thoughts and memories that she hardly sees the world changing around her. When Tina and her Dad stop in a small town that hasn't changed much since 1918, it's a chance for her thoughts and memories to shuffle into an order that might make a little more sense.

New from Doublejoy Books is the short novel *Plum Tree*, a story of transition from place to place and time to time. There's no fanfare or surprise when Tina meets young Tim, who lost his mother to the

1. https://books2read.com/u/boEZ10

2. https://books2read.com/u/boEZ10

Spanish flu. As she shifts from childhood to youth, from present to past and future, she's thinking of how to connect her music with people. As Tina says, *Local stories. There could be a lot of them, especially if you didn't need them to be about guns and crimes but maybe about sports or inventing things. Or just ordinary life but as if it counted.*

Read more at books2read.com/paulaj.

Also by Paula Johanson

Prime Ministers of Canada
Pierre Elliott Trudeau: Child of Nature
Charles Tupper: Warhorse

Slice of Life
No Parent Is An Island
Working Parent
Under The Plow

Young Science
Bat Poop Sparkles

Standalone
Small Rain and Other Nightmares
Island Views
Plum Tree
Tower in the Crooked Wood

King Kwong: Larry Kwong, the China Clipper Who Broke the NHL
Colour Barrier
Woolgathering: Awareness of the Foreign in Published Works About
Cowichan Woolworking
Science Critters
Green Paddler

Watch for more at books2read.com/paulaj.

About the Author

Paula Johanson is a Canadian writer. A graduate of the University of Victoria with an MA in Canadian literature, she has worked as a security guard, a short order cook, a teacher, newspaper writer, and more. As well as editing books and teaching materials, she has run an organic-method small farm with her spouse, raised gifted twins, and cleaned university dormitories. In addition to novels and stories, she is the author of forty-two books written for educational publishers, among them *The Paleolithic Revolution* and *Women Writers* from the series *Defying Convention: Women Who Changed The World*. Johanson is an active member of SF Canada, the national association of science fiction and fantasy authors.

Read more at books2read.com/paulaj.

About the Publisher

Doublejoy Books is the publisher of a variety of eclectic books of Canadian literature.

http://doublejoybooks.com

http://books2read.com/paulaj

www.ingramcontent.com/pod-product-compliance
Lightning Source LLC
Chambersburg PA
CBHW022052170626
46808CB00003B/1445